Meeting Mi[...]

Carol Ann Duffy was born in Glasgow in 1955. She has published five collections of poems for adults and has received many awards, including a Somerset M[...] Award [...] Cholmond[...] of poems, *Mean Time*, won [...] poetry and the Forward Prize for [...] recent collection is *The World's Wife*. She has edited two anthologies of poems for young readers and is currently completing a third.

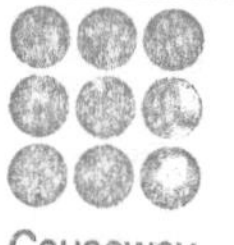

by the same author

Rumplestiltskin and Other Grimm Tales

poetry for adults

Standing Female Nude
Selling Manhattan
The Other Country
Mean Time
Selected Poems
The World's Wife

as editor

I Wouldn't Thank You for a Valentine
Stopping for Death

CAROL ANN DUFFY

Meeting Midnight

with illustrations by Eileen Cooper

faber and faber

First published in 1999
by Faber and Faber Limited
3 Queen Square London WC1N 3AU

Typeset by Faber and Faber
Printed in England by MPG Books Limited,
Victoria Square, Bodmin, Cornwall

A CIP record for this book
is available from the British Library

ISBN 0-571-20120-2

10 9 8 7 6 5 4 3 2

for Ella with love from mummy

Contents

Cucumbers
♫ ♫
The Invention of Rain
Time Transfixed *by René Magritte*
A Child's Sleep

Meeting Midnight

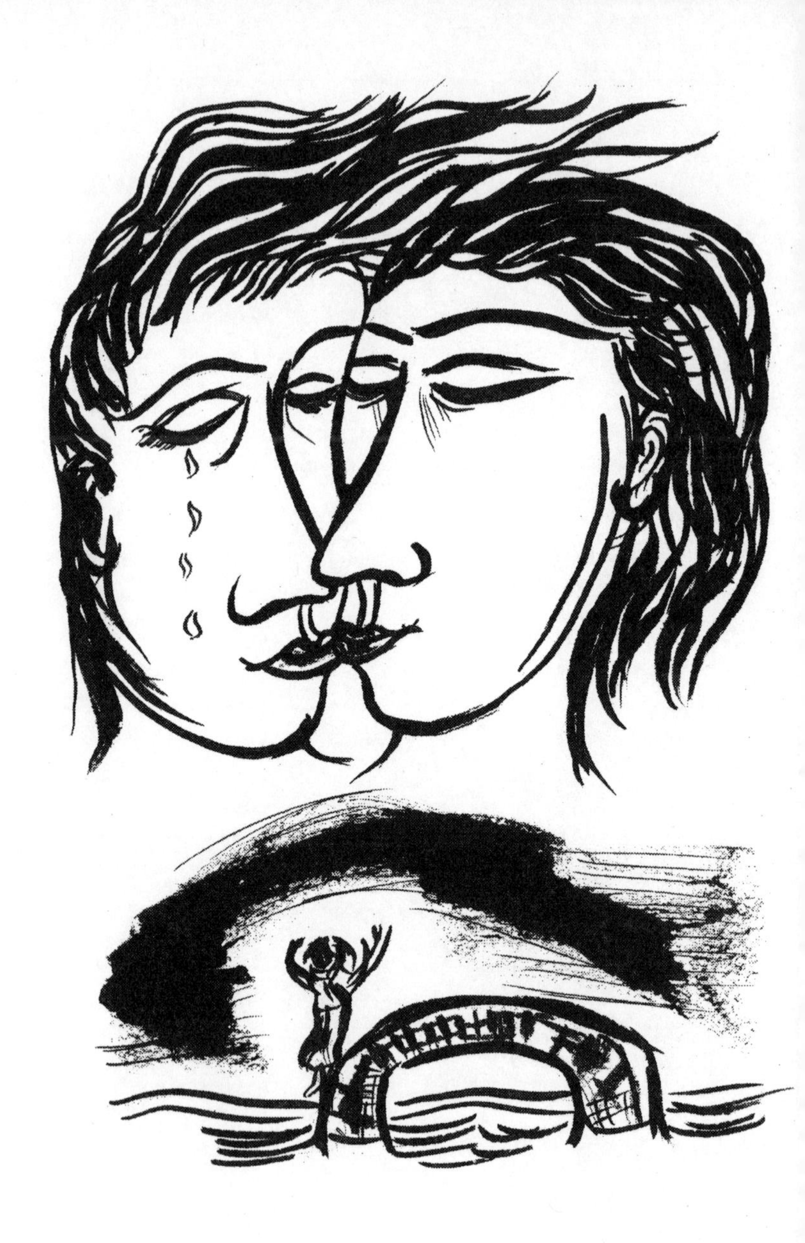

Meeting Midnight

I met Midnight.
Her eyes were sparkling pavements after frost.
She wore a full-length, dark-blue raincoat with a hood.
She winked. She smoked a small cheroot.

I followed her.
Her walk was more a shuffle, more a dance.
She took the path to the river, down she went.
On Midnight's scent,
I heard the twelve cool syllables, her name,
chime from the town.
When those bells stopped,

Midnight paused by the water's edge.
She waited there.
I saw a girl in purple on the bridge.
It was One o'Clock.
Hurry, Midnight said. *It's late, it's late.*
I saw them run together.
Midnight wept.
They kissed full on the lips
and then I slept.

The next day I bumped into Half-Past Four.
He was a bore.

Late

She was eight. She was out late.
She bounced a tennis ball homewards before her
in the last of the light.
She'd been warned. She'd been told. It grew cold.
She took a shortcut through the churchyard.
She was a small child
making her way home. She was quite brave.
She fell into an open grave.

It was deep. It was damp. It smelled strange.
Help, she cried, *Help, it's Me*! She shouted
her own name.
Nobody came.
The churchbells tolled sadly. Shame. Shame.

She froze. She had a blue nose.
She clapped her hands.
She stamped her feet in soft, slip-away soil.
She hugged herself. Her breath was a ghost
floating up from a grave.
Then she prayed.

But only the moon stared down
with its callous face.
Only the spiteful stars sniggered, far out in space.
Only the gathering clouds
threw down a clap of thunder

like an ace.
And her, she was eight, going on nine.
She was late.

Questions, Questions

Why is my shadow copying me?
Because you are right.
Why do bananas smile in their bowl?
Because of your kind bite.

Why is the moon following me?
Because of your p-p-peep.
Why do the stars giggle at me?
Because of your h-h-hop.

Why do the trees gossip and nudge?
Because you are News.
How shall I find my way home in the dark?
By the light of your yellow shoes.

Lies

I like to go out for the day and tell lies.
The day should be overcast
with a kind of purple, electric edge to the clouds;
and not too hot or cold,
but cool.
I turn up the collar of my coat
and narrow my eyes.

I meet someone –
a girl from school perhaps –
I like them shy.
Then I start to lie
as we walk along Tennyson Drive kicking a can.
She listens hard,
her split strawberry mouth moist and mute;
my weasel words
sparking the little lights in her spectacles.
At the corner of Coleridge Place
I watch her run,
thrilled, fast, chasing her breath,
home to her mum.

Bus-stops I like,
with long, bored, footsore, moaning queues.
I lie to them
in my shrill, confident voice,
till the number 8 or 11 takes them away

and I stand and stare at the bend in Longfellow Road,
alone in the day.

At the end of the darkening afternoon
I head for home,
watching the lights turn on in truthful rooms
where mothers come and go
with plates of cakes,
and TV sets shuffle their bright cartoons.
Then I knock on the door of 21 Wordsworth Way,
and while I wait
I watch a spaceship zoom away overhead
and see the faint half-smile of the distant moon.
They let me in.
And who, they want to know, do I think I am?
Exactly where have I been? With whom? And why?
The thing with me –
I like to come home after a long day out
and lie.

Prior Knowledge

Prior Knowledge was a strange boy.
He had sad green eyes.
He always seemed to know when I was telling lies.

We were friends for a summer.
Prior got out his knife
and mixed our bloods so we'd be brothers for life.

You'll be rich, he said, and famous;
but I must die.
Then brave, clever Prior began to cry.

He knew so much.
He knew the day before
I'd drop a jamjar full of frogspawn on the kitchen floor.

He knew there were wasps
in the gardening gloves.
He knew the name of the girl I'd grow up to love.

The day he died
he knew there would be
a wind shaking conkers from the horse-chestnut tree;

and an aimless child
singing down Prior's street,
with bright red sandals on her skipping feet.

Know All

I know something you don't know.
I know what you mean.
I know what's going on round here.
I know what I've seen.
I know the score.
I know a lot more
than folk give me credit for.
I know what's what.
I know a lot.
I know all that.

I know the lay of the land.
I know it like I know
the back of my own hand.
I know enough.
I know my stuff.
I know what you're saying.
I know which way the wind
is blowing.
I know what to do.
I know who's who.

I know the ropes.
I know the ins and outs.
I know my onions.
I know what folk are on about.
I know beyond a shadow of a doubt –

I DON'T KNOW NOWT.

Whee!

I held my head in both my hands
and flung it through the air.
Blown by the wind, it flew away,
streaming out my hair.

The world, from high perspectives, looked
duller than ditchwater.
I rose above all mundane things –
Halley's Comet's daughter.

Higher than the flightpath of dreams
my cranium sped on;
while, down below, the people shrieked
'She's crazy! Head's gone.'

It's easy. Just shrug your shoulders,
turn your mind to the sky;
then throw your head like a basket-ball.
Wheee! Goodbye. Goodbye . . .

Little Ghost

Think of me as a child
who has swallowed herself whole –
gulp, gone –
leaving only
the colour of goat's cheese,
the hue of a buried bone,
the tint of the last dab of vanilla ice-cream
in a cone.

I'm all alone
in the Library
with the old books;
have been for ages.
My smoky fingers can't turn the pages.
I'm so-o-o bored.
I make a portrait fall
from the wall
to the floor – CRASH –
in one of my sudden rages.
Scary. Spooky. Totally freaky.
I pipe my thin spirit noise
on the limy-lemony air.
Ooooooooo. Creepy.

I’m not here, not there,
untouched, unheard, unseen.
Think of me as a film
escaped from a screen,
a has-been,
an absolute scream.

Think of me as a late guest,
a gust of wind,
dancing dust on the air.
What is my name? Can you guess?
Do you know, you foolish scared creature?
My name is Little Ghost.

Poker

A skeleton
on the sea-bed,
a bullet-hole
in its bone head.

Three queens
in its claw hand,
a black ace
on the pale sand.

A fish swims
near a fourth queen
where a shirt sleeve
would once have been.

Queens

A cold, bored Queen lived in a castle.
She was Queen as far as the castle walls,
no farther.
Rooks flapped about. HM stared out from the East tower
in her blue robes, in the dull old gold of her crown;
a thin white Queen with grey-green eyes under a tight frown.

She wrote to a second Queen; she penned a formal letter
with a clammy candlewax seal. *I hope*
you are feeling better. Please come.
For three days, a man on a black horse
rode uphill with the letter.
For two days, he rode downhill with the answer.
Very well. Very well.
A trembling royal hand reached out, tugged
at the hanging rope of the servants' bell.

Queen Two was fat, with a loud voice
and a temper.
She dressed in a piccalilli yellow.
Queen One came down to greet her
in the Great Pink Hall for dinner.
Clear soup. Spinach. Fish.
What's this? the big Queen bellowed,
Rubbish to make me thinner?
Where is the curry, the pepper, the pickle,
the onion, the mustard and chilli?

Where is the garlic bread?
I'm off to bed.

At daybreak, a quiet Queen sat by her chessboard,
pale, apprehensive, fainter of heart.
A cross Queen thumped in, unthin.
What's going on? Where are the boxing-gloves,
the duelling swords, the snooker cues, where are the darts?
The rooks outside were alarmed, cawed back
at her deafening shout –
I'M GOING OUT!

That night, Queen One mooted a walk
in the castle grounds.
It was mild. There was a moon up above
and a moon in the moat.
They could stroll, calm, polite, Queen hand in Queen glove,
under the yews, the ancient oaks.
Is this a joke? Queen Two snapped.
Where are the bagpipes, the fiddlers three,
where is the karaoke? Answer me that!
TAXI!

So both Queens tried harder, harder.
Queen Thin let Queen Fat
raid the royal larder.
Fat held Thin's wool,

her big, plump, soft regal hands
frozen mid-clap.
Queen Thin knitted away, click, click-clack, click-clack.
Then both Queens sat in a marble bath –
Fat at the bottom, Thin by the taps –

We are clean Queens, they sang,
We are fragrant.
We are very very very clean Queens.

And when it was time,
Queen One managed a slight bow of the head,
Queen Two shuffled the start of a curtsy
under her dress.
Farewell, farewell,
a fat Queen called from a gold coach,
trotting away down the gravel drive, over the moat,
a big puce Queen
with a string of rubies at her throat.
Goodbye, goodbye.

Goodbye. A thin Queen waved from a window, shyly,
then fingered her new pearls.
One two three four five six seven.
Seven rooks round a castle started to cry.

Boys

1 Paul

I wake early, gargle with my bells
to shake out birds from my stone curls.
My thoughts are gargoyles.

I can see the river with my stained-glass eyes,
the boats and barges floating like ideas.
My huge forehead frowns in London skies.

I'm cold, but I do not mind the cold.
Far away, I hear the stammered prayers of the healed.
Far away, I hear the baptised crying of a child.

2 Oscar

Give me the hands of Marlon Brando.
Give me the neck of Gregory Peck.
Give me the smile of Robert de Niro.
Give me the brain of John Wayne.

Give me the eyes of Bette Davis.
Give me the hair of Cher.
Give me the legs of Betty Grable.
Give me it all one more time. I was there.

3 Stanley

I'm a flashing blade, I'm a knave.
A fork's my wife.
I'll make my point – enough's enough.
I'll cut up rough.
I'll cut your coat according to your cloth.
I'll cut no ice.
Cross me, you're blind, dumb, deaf,
a stiff.
I'll have your life,
like this, quick – *Knife* . . .

4 Gordon Bennett

Is it uncouth?
Is it a fate worse than death?
Is it like coal in the bath?

Is it a kick in the teeth?
Is it a just cause for wrath?
Is it like having bad breath?

When your ******* *** name is a ******* **** oath.

5 Ben

I'm big,
bigger than fifty men.
I go Dong! Dong! Dong! Dong! Dong!
Dong! Dong! Dong! Dong! Dong!
on *News at Ten.*

Elvis Lives

Elvis lives.
He's in my class at school.
He's cool.
He walks across the playground,
swirls his hips.
He sings hymns in assembly,
curls his lip.

Elvis is alive
and well.
He took a piece of chalk
and on the blackboard
while the teacher took a walk
wrote out the lyrics of
Heartbreak Hotel.

Elvis talks.
He did not die.
He's top in Maths.
He's good at swimming, French and cookery,
good for a laugh.
He wears school uniform, school tie,
school blue suede shoes.
He keeps his head down when he's got the blues

or, by the bike shed,
plays an air guitar.

Love Me Tender
on the playground air.
My best friend, Elvis Presley, with his slicked-back hair.

Jemima Riddle

A:
Jemima Riddle
plays the fiddle,
hey-diddle-diddle
d.

B:
D'you think the kid'll
play the middle
bit of it at
t?

A:
No. Jemima Riddle'
d rather piddle,
hey-diddle-diddle –
d.

B:
P?

A:
Oui. But a quid'll
stop the widdle,
then she'll fiddle –
C?

Lightning Star

for May Duffy and her eleven grandchildren

I run at Lightning Star
and mount her back in one smooth jump;
then gallop her down Rising Brook,
wind in my face.
My pigtails thump.

My trusty steed.
I bend low to her ear
as trees rush by in camouflage.
We fly,
her coconut hooves racing with my heart
towards Moss Pit.

My piebald mount.
My equine brave.
My speed of light.
My warrior.
My Lightning Star.

It isn't far
to where we live –
21 Poplar Way –
so I slow down
as we approach the giant trees
which guard our neat estate.
I'm saddle-sore.
I stand up in my stirrups.

Time for bed.
I feel my horse's handlebars against my knees.
I hear my horse's neighing in my head.

Snowball

More snow fell that week
than had fallen for thirty years.
The cold squeezed like a bully's hug
and made you grin at nothing.

Andrew Pond and Davy Rickers and me
went out,
three sprats,
into the white bite of the world.
We shared my balaclava.

And for an hour we chucked snowballs
at the windows on our estate;
spattered the pristine panes of Nelson Way,
powdered the gleaming glass up Churchill Drive,
until we got bored
and Andrew Pond's mitts from his Granny
shrank.

It was me who started it off,
that last snowball,
rolling it from the size of a 50p scoop
down Thatcher Hill
to the size of a spacehopper.
It creaked under my gloves as I pushed.
Then Andrew Pond and Davy Rickers joined in,
and we shoved the thing

the length of Wellington Road.
It groaned as it grew
and grew.

The size of a sleeping polar bear.
The size of an igloo.
The size,
by the time we turned the corner
into the road where I lived,
of a full moon –
the three of us astronauts.

The worst of it was
that Andrew Pond and Davy Rickers ran off,
leaving me
dwarfed and alarmed
by a planet of snow
on our front lawn.
It went so dark in our living-room,
I was later to hear,
that my mother thought there had been an eclipse.

And later that night –
after the terrible telling-off,
red-eyed,
supperless –
I stared from my bedroom window

at the enormity of my crime,
huge and luminous
under the ice-cold stars.
To tell the truth,
it was pride that I felt,
even though
I had to stop in for as long as it took
for the snowball to melt.

The Duke of Fire and the Duchess of Ice

Passionate love for the Duke of Fire
the Duchess of Ice felt.
One kiss was her heart's desire,
but with one kiss she would melt.

She dreamed of him in his red pantaloons,
in his orange satin blouse,
in his crimson cravat,
in his tangerine hat,
in his vermilion dancing shoes.

One kiss, one kiss,
lips of flame on frost,
one kiss, pure bliss,
and never count the cost.

She woke. She went to the bathroom.
She took a freezing shower –
her body as pale as a stalagmite,
winter's frailest flower.

Then the Duke of Fire stood there,
radiant, ablaze with love,
and the Duchess of Ice cared nothing
for anything in the world.

She spoke his name,
her voice was snow,
kissed him, kissed him again,
and in his warm, passionate arms
turned to water, tears, rain.

Whirlpool

I saw two hands in the whirlpool
clutching at air,
but when I knelt by the swirling edge
nothing was there.
Behind me, twelve tall green-black trees shook
and scattered their rooks.
I turned to the spinning waters again
and looked.

I saw two legs in the whirlpool
dancing deep.
I see that horrible choreography still
in my turning sleep.
Then I heard the dog from Field o' Blood Farm
howl on its chain;
and gargling out from the whirlpool came the watery sound
of a name.

I bent my head to the whirlpool,
I saw a face,
Then I knew that I should run for my life
away from that place.
But my eyes and mouth were opening wide, far below
as I drowned.
And the words I tell were silver fish
the day I was found.

Girl and Tree

A girl fell in love with a tree
and a tree with a girl.
Holding the tree in her arms, the girl said
Tree, I love you best in the world.
Why, said the tree, *do you love me so?*
Because of the green of your leaves, said the girl.

The girl climbed up into the tree
and sat on a branch, dangling her legs.
Girl, girl, I love you best, believe me please,
whispered the tree.
Why, said the girl, *do you love best me?*
Because of your cherry-red dress, said the tree.

Then the wind blew and the tree's green sails
breathed and gasped and filled with air
and the wood of the tree creaked like a ship
and the girl was Captain there.

Only the moon, agog with light,
saw the girl and the tree that night
when the whole town, in full pursuit,
came with dogs and searched the woods
where a smiling girl in a cherry-red dress
slept in the arms of a tree, like fruit.

Star and Moon

for Helen Taylor

An unborn child slept
in the gleam of a star.
A childless mother tossed and turned
on a moon.
High over the moon
the chuckling light of the star.
Beneath the star
the milky glow of the moon.

An unborn child
fell through the dark
like a shooting star.
A mother held out her arms
on the highest hill of the moon.
There you are!
Yes, I am coming soon!
Little Star singing to Mama Moon.

Then a child was born
and she slept
on the breast of the moon.
And a mother's arms were filled
with the light of a star.
Everything far comes near,
sang the moon to the star,
and everything near goes far.

First Summer

Here is your shadow-hand
holding the shadow of mine
as we drift along
over the grass
after a bee
or a butterfly.
You shout their names.
And here are the shadows
of your first words,
seen through the throat of a flower.

Here is a ball
bouncing away,
yellow and yellow,
under the sun;
your unwrapped voice
calling it back.
Here is a sun-hat,
blue and green,
a melting cone
in your fist.
And here is a message
faxed from the heart
to the lips,
as my shadow kneels again beside yours
for a shadow-kiss.

Sharp Freckles

for Ben Simmons

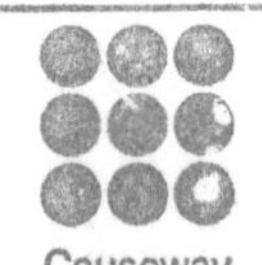

He picks me up, his big thumbs under my armpits tickle,
then puts me down. On his belt there is a shining silver
buckle.
I hold his hand and see, close up, the dark hairs on his
knuckles.

He sings to me. His voice is loud and funny and I giggle.
Now we will eat. I listen to my breakfast as it crackles.
He nods and smiles. His eyes are birds in little nests of
wrinkles.

We kick a ball, red and white, between us. When he tackles
I'm on the ground, breathing a world of grass. It prickles.
He bends. He lifts me high above his head. Frightened, I
wriggle.

Face to his face, I watch the sweat above each caterpillar-
eyebrow trickle.
He rubs his nose on mine, once, twice, three times, and we
both chuckle.
He hasn't shaved today. He kisses me. He has sharp freckles.

So Shy

He was so shy he was born with a caul,
sort of a shawl made from the membrane
of the womb. He was tongue-tied;

so shy he kept a dummy in his mouth
for two years; then, when that went,
a thumb. He was wide-eyed, dumb; so shy

he would hide in the cupboard under the stairs
for hours, with a bear; hearing his name called
from the top to the bottom of the house, quiet

as a mouse; shy as the milk in a coconut,
shy as a slither of soap. When he got dressed,
he wore shy clothes – a balaclava, mitts.

He ate shy food – blancmange, long-lasting mints.
He drank shy drinks – juice from a cup
with a lid and a lip, sip by shy sip.

He was so shy he lived with a blush,
sort of a flush under the skin, like the light
behind curtains on windows when somebody's in.

Toy Dog

for Matthew Kay

When I come home from school, he doesn't bark.
He doesn't fetch the stick I throw for him in Clissold Park,
or bite a burglar's ankle in the dark.
Toy dog.

When I wake up he doesn't lick my face.
He never beats me by a mile the times we have a race,
or digs a bone up from his secret place.
Toy dog.

When I say *Heel!* or *Sit!* he can't obey.
I buy a red dog-collar for him, though he will not stray,
or trip me up at soccer when I play.
Toy dog.

One day his brown glass eyes will soften, see.
One night, his nylon tail will wag when I come in for tea;
his cloth leg cock against a lamp-post for a pee.
Good dog.

The Childminders

I was six when I went to see
if a brace of childminders
would suit small me.

They lived where the sun
couldn't quite reach.
A corner house. Number 101.

One childminder was tall, stooped, thin,
and three or four teeth
short of a grin.

Childminder Two was of smaller build,
with boiled red eyes.
My blood chilled.

They had one toy. They had one book.
They said: *Here, little girl,*
have a good look.

The toy was a broken clockwork mouse.
The book was as dusty
as the gloomy house.

I'm afraid I won't require you, I smiled
and backed away. Then I saw,
to my horror, a skeletal child –

slumped in the corner, bored to death.
There but for the grace of god . . .
I thought, and left.

A Worry

It's come to live in my room – a worry.
I asked when was it planning to leave?
It said it was in no particular hurry.
It's not slimy and it's not furry.
It's not clammy and it's not hairy.
I can't describe it.
When I whip round to stare it straight
in the eye, it's not there.
But believe me,
if there's one thing I know for certain, for sure,
I know that the worry's there.

It hunkers down. It squats.
Its breathing swaps the colour of my room
from cheerful to gloom. The curtains look drawn.
The bed is a wreck.
My face in the mirror looks like a vampire's had a takeaway
from the neck.
It's there at dawn – the worry.
I've told it I'm too young to marry!
I want to be free!
No no no no no, it said,
I belong to it forever and it belongs to me.

Help! Au secours! Mayday!
What can I do?
Will anyone credit the size the worry has grown to?

A rat. A mongrel. A puma. An ape. A creature from Mars.
Can anyone hear the sound of the worry's voice?
A wasp. Slow handclaps. A dentist's drill. The squealing brakes
of skidding cars.
And what about other girls?
What about boys?
Do they have worry growing like fungi
over their books and toys?

Now life is hell.
Life is a horrid trick.
I'm worried sick.

Quicksand

Mrs Leather's told you about quicksand;
now you're scared.
You'd take the short-cut through the muddy field
if you dared.

But quicksand takes a laced-up shoe,
a white sock,
then sips a trembling pair of knees.
Its moist suck

drinks the hem of a new blue dress
to the waist.
Your hands will panic over your head,
claw at space.

Quicksand under your armpits, up to your chin.
Now you drown
the way Mrs Leather said you would.
The whole town

comes searching, searching with blankets and lights.
But too late –
only your satchel's found, at dawn, at the edge of the field
by this gate.

Five Girls

Philomena Cooney
wears green sandals,
yellow ribbons,
silver bangles;
knows three secrets,
lives in a tent
in the middle of a field
near the River Trent.

Arabella Murkhi
speaks in Latin,
keeps her cat in,
sleeps in satin.
Went to Turkey
just like that.
Absolutely *loved* it.
Amo amas amat.

Isadora Dooley
loves her jewellery.
Pearls on Sundays,
diamonds Mondays,
rubies Tuesdays,
Wednesdays blue days,
Thursday Friday Saturdays
it-doesn't-really-matter days.

Esther Feaver,
opera diva
dressed in beaver,
loved a weaver;
took a breather,
grabbed a cleaver,
now the weaver
will not leave her.

Joan Stone
liked a good moan,
lived on her own
in a mobile home.
The doorbell never rang,
neither did the phone;
so she pressed her ear
to the dialling tone.

Chocs

Into the half-pound box of Moonlight
my small hand crept.
There was an electrifying rustle.
There was a dark and glamorous scent.
Into my open, religious mouth
the first Marzipan Moment went.

Down in the crinkly second layer
five finger-piglets snuffled
among the Hazelnut Whirl,
the Caramel Swirl,
the Black Cherry and Almond Truffle.

Bliss.

I chomped, I gorged.
I stuffed my face,
till only the Coffee Cream
was left for the owner of the box –
tough luck, Ann Pope –
oh, and half an Orange Supreme.

Cucumbers

Money is cucumbers now.
My mother earns twenty thousand a year.
Cucumbers don't grow on trees, she snaps,
but gives me four of them each week,
two for each deep pocket of my winter coat,
pocket-money.

Folk keep their cucumbers in banks.
Innumerable cucumbers,
cool and green,
in the ice-cold, deep-freeze safes.
Some folk are millionaires,
they own so many.

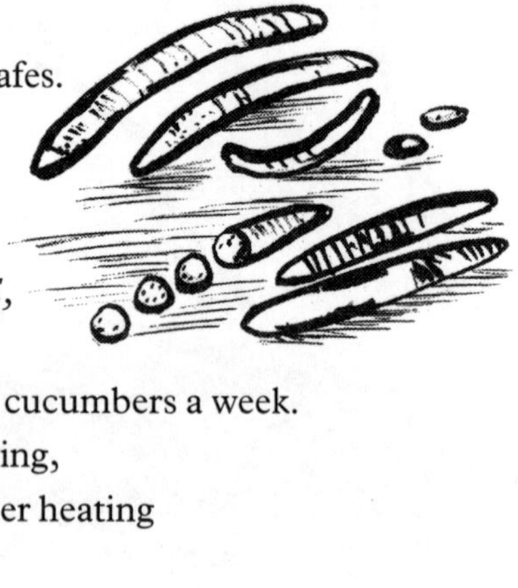

More cucumbers than SENSE,
my grandmother shouts.
She has a state pension of 58 cucumbers a week.
Although it is snowing, snowing,
she is frightened to turn up her heating
because of the cost.

My teacher writes:
On what could you spend one hundred cucumbers?
My mind goes blank.
I stare at the empty page of my exercise book
for a long time
with my shiny, pale-green eyes.

♫ ♫

The piano eats with chop sticks,
cool minims,
diced demi-semiquavers.

When the lid goes down,
the piano is inscrutable,
shining with health.

The piano stands politely
until the next meal, silent
for as long as it takes.

The Invention of Rain

Rain first came
when the woman whose lovely face
was the sky
cried.

She thought of rain
for her sadness,
her sorrowful clouds.
The woman whose lonely voice
was the wind
howled.

Then garden flowers
bowed their heads
under the soft-salt grief of the rain.

And an only child
stared down at them
through the thousand tears
of a window-pane.

Time Transfixed

by René Magritte

In the Thinking Room
at Childhood Hall,
the brown clock ticks
with the sound of the kiss
that my Grandma makes
against my cheek
again and again
when we first meet
after a week
of all the hours
that the brown clock's tick
has kissed away
today, to-
morrow, yesterday

are all the same
to the plum steam-train
that I sometimes hear
in the Thinking Room
at Childhood Hall –
it has no passengers at all,
till I grow old enough
and tall
to climb aboard
the plum steam-train
and blow a kiss
as I chuff away to to-
morrow, yesterday, today.

A Child's Sleep

I stood at the edge of my child's sleep
hearing her breathe;
although I could not enter there,
I could not leave.

Her sleep was a small wood,
perfumed with flowers;
dark, peaceful, sacred,
acred in hours.

And she was the spirit that lives
in the heart of such woods;
without time, without history,
wordlessly good.

I spoke her name, a pebble dropped
in the still night,
and saw her stir, both open palms
cupping their soft light;

then went to the window. The greater dark
outside the room
gazed back, maternal, wise,
with its face of moon.